Laugh your Socks off with

Jeremy STRONG

Krankenstein's Crazy House of Horror

Illustrated by Rowan Clifford

PUFFIN

PUFFIN BOOKS

Published by the Penguin Group
Penguin Books Ltd, 80 Strand, London WC2R 0RL, England
Penguin Group (USA) Inc., 375 Hudson Street, New York, New York 10014, USA
Penguin Group (Canada), 90 Eglinton Avenue East, Suite 700, Toronto, Ontario, Canada M4P 2Y3
(a division of Pearson Penguin Canada Inc.)
Penguin Ireland, 25 St Stephen's Green, Dublin 2, Ireland (a division of Penguin Books Ltd)
Penguin Group (Australia), 250 Camberwell Road, Camberwell, Victoria 3124, Australia
(a division of Pearson Australia Group Pty Ltd)
Penguin Books India Pvt Ltd, 11 Community Centre, Panchsheel Park, New Delhi – 110 017, India
Penguin Group (NZ), 67 Apollo Drive, Rosedale, North Shore 0632, New Zealand
(a division of Pearson New Zealand Ltd)
Penguin Books (South Africa) (Pty) Ltd, 24 Sturdee Avenue, Rosebank, Johannesburg 2196, South Africa

Penguin Books Ltd, Registered Offices: 80 Strand, London WC2R 0RL, England

puffinbooks.com

First published 2009
1

Text copyright © Jeremy Strong, 2009
Illustrations copyright © Rowan Clifford, 2009
All rights reserved

The moral right of the author and illustrator has been asserted

Set in Baskerville
Made and printed in England by Clays Ltd, St Ives plc

British Library Cataloguing in Publication Data
A CIP catalogue record for this book is available from the British Library

ISBN: 978-0-141-32499-9

www.greenpenguin.co.uk

Mixed Sources
Product group from well-managed
forests and other controlled sources
www.fsc.org Cert no. SA-COC-1592
© 1996 Forest Stewardship Council

Penguin Books is committed to a sustainable future
for our business, our readers and our planet.
The book in your hands is made from paper
certified by the Forest Stewardship Council.

Thanks to all my family for the laughter,
the meals, the advice (even if I didn't want any!)
and their great company over many years.
You have given me everything The Stitcher never had.

Contents

1 A Bit Before the Beginning

'Crumblebag lives in a cave,' sniggered Charlie, but his great pal Ben shook his head.

'No, in a wheelie bin,' he declared. 'It's all dark and wet and smelly inside and she eats worms and earwiggy things that hide in the slime and she makes her clothes out of rotten cabbage leaves. That's why she stinks of cabbage.'

It was a good thing that Mrs Rumble (commonly known in school

as Crumblebag) couldn't hear the two boys, because Mrs Rumble was their teacher. She certainly *didn't* live in a cave or a wheelie bin and she didn't eat worms and grubs either. However, she *did* smell of cabbage, which was unfortunate but true.

Ben was staying with Charlie for the weekend. He liked Charlie's house because it was a bit manic. This was probably because Charlie had three sisters, all younger than him. Between them, the three sisters produced the same kind of energy you might find at an explosion in a firework factory. Ben was a bit manic himself

so he fitted into the general pattern pretty well.

It was Charlie who was different. He preferred a quiet life, without surprises. Beneath a frantic nest of unruly black hair he had large, startled eyes. Charlie was startled by many things. A bird flying past in the distance might well cause a sharp exclamation – 'Ooh!' – as if he'd just escaped being carried off by a blackbird and being fed to her young. (In Charlie's imagination blackbirds were obviously the size of aircraft.)

Ben, on the other hand, was always dashing around as if his pants were on fire, which did actually happen to him once, but that's another story. He was always getting in and, sometimes, out of trouble. If Charlie's sisters  were like a firework explosion then Ben was the biggest banger among them. His mother liked it when Ben went to stay at Charlie's because it gave her with some peace and quiet for a change.

Now the two boys were spending the weekend

together and they were facing a big problem.
Mrs Rumble had set some homework for the
whole class.

'I want you all to write a story,' she had told
her disgruntled brood of ten-year-olds. 'We've
written made-up stories and now I want you to
write a true story, about yourselves.'

Charlie had gone home with the grumps. That
was a bad thing, considering it was Friday and he
had the whole weekend ahead, so he should have
been as happy as a cheetah with rollerblades.
But by the time they were getting ready for bed
Charlie had worked himself into a real blue
mood.

'I've got nothing to write about,' he
complained to Ben. 'Nothing interesting ever
happens.'

Ben began leaping up and down on Charlie's
bed, trying to make his head touch the ceiling.
'Why not write a story about child slaves in
Victorian times? You know, like Mrs Crumble

was telling us in assembly the other day. And Charles Dickens could come along and save them all, like Superman, only with a top hat and a big beard.'

Charlie rolled his eyes. 'Charles Dickens was not a superhero, he was just a Victorian writer.'

'Yeah, but he still went and helped stop child slavery,' insisted Ben.

'He didn't wear his underpants on top of his trousers and whizz through the air, did he?' Charlie argued.

'Didn't say he did,' Ben answered. 'I said he was *like* Superman. Didn't say he was.'

Charlie shook his head and refused to cheer up. 'It wouldn't be a true story, though, would it?'

'Well, it would, sort of. Ow!' Ben had finally hit the ceiling. He sat down heavily on Charlie's bed.

'Anyhow,' Charlie grumbled, 'Crumblebag said it had to be a true story about *me*. I'm not an ancient Victorian. I'm just me in the twenty-first century and, like I said, nothing interesting ever happens to me.'

Ben grinned. 'Crumblebag didn't say it had to be interesting.'

'What's the point of writing a story if it's not interesting?' Charlie moaned.

'Doesn't matter,' insisted his friend. 'She just said true. Just write something you did.'

'Great. So I'll put this then: *One day I went home from school. Then I had some tea. It was fish and chips. Then I watched some television. Then I went upstairs. I got into bed. Then I went to sleep. The End.*'

Ben grinned. 'Exactly. It's a true story. But you missed out what happened after that.'

'What do you mean? Nothing happened afterwards,' Charlie grumbled.

'Of course it did. You showed Crumblebag your story and she told you off for being boring and starting sentences with "then".' Ben grinned at Charlie.

'Ha ha, very funny. You know what I mean, it's

not a story. Nothing happens. Things happen in proper stories.'

Ben shrugged and said that he had plenty to write about. 'Things are always happening to me,' he claimed.

Charlie ignored him. That didn't help at all. He struggled into the new pyjamas his mother had bought him.

'Whoa!' cried Ben, who was now attempting a complete mid-air somersault on Charlie's bed. He came crashing down on his back. 'What are you WEARING? They are WEIRD!'

'No they're not, they're cool,' said Charlie defensively.

'Yeah, AND weird! What are all those pictures meant to be?'

Charlie answered with a shrug and together they peered at all the little pictures that covered the pyjamas from top to toe.

'Where did you get them?' asked Ben. 'I want a pair. They're great. I LOVE those pics!'

'Mum got them from a charity shop. She says they're Cosmic Pyjamas. That's what the label inside reckons.'

'Cosmic Pyjamas,' Ben repeated softly, examining the pictures more closely. 'Weird. There are planets and little people, houses, castles, animals and kings, forests and pyramids and mountains and everything.'

'I know,' nodded Charlie, and he quietly added that looking at the pictures sometimes made his spine tingle.

'Tingle?' Ben glanced at his friend. 'That's –'

'Weird!' they chorused, setting about each other with Charlie's pillows, until Charlie suddenly clutched Ben's arm.

'Stop! Look!'

'What?'

Charlie pointed at his left leg. His eyes were almost popping out of his head. The colour had drained from his face and he was as white as a pickled egg.

'The picture moved,' he croaked.

'What picture?' asked Ben.

'That one. The dark house.'

'Don't be daft. Pictures don't move.' Ben pushed his friend jokily but Charlie didn't smile.

'It moved, Ben. I saw it. Definitely.'

The two boys bent over the pyjamas, staring at the picture. Ben knew that Charlie was easily panicked and he gently teased him.

'It looks like a haunted house to me,' he said casually, giving Charlie a nudge. 'It's a creepy heapy full of sneaky beakies!'

'I'm not listening,' Charlie said. 'You're just trying to wind me up.'

Ben sat up straight. 'It's only a picture on your pyjamas, Charlie. It's cool.'

But Charlie didn't think it was cool at all. He didn't like haunted houses, and he certainly didn't like having pictures that moved on his pyjamas.

'So what did it do that was so scary?' asked Ben.

'It sort of wriggled, like it was shivering.'

Ben grinned and studied the house once more. He wiggled his fingers and dropped his voice as low as possible. 'It's the Haunted House of Jelly, and it's Terribly Jellibly Smelly,' he murmured and then, as he finished – *Fwissssssss!* A tiny bolt of lightning briefly lit the dark clouds behind the house.

Ben leaped back as if he'd been bitten. 'Wow! Did you see that?'

Charlie nodded. His heart was pounding and his throat so dry he couldn't speak. This was getting way too creepy. But Ben was fascinated. He bent over the pyjamas once more. Another flash of lightning slammed between the clouds, lighting up the mysterious mansion.

'It did it again!' cried Ben. 'There was a flash of lightning right there!' he yelled, stabbing a finger at Charlie's leg.

BANGG! KERRANNGGG!!
PHWOOOOOSSHHH!!!

The moment he touched the picture the world disappeared – at least that's what it seemed like to the boys. In an instant they found themselves tumbling through space, with giant lightning bolts of sizzling colour shooting around them as they clung to each other, screaming with fear. On and on they went, falling, spinning, arms and legs flailing until suddenly –

WHUMMPPP! OUCH!!
KER-SPLOSSHHH!!!

Charlie went sprawling across a slippery floor, while Ben found himself plunging head first into a giant basin full of tomato soup.

2 The Stitcher and a Volcano on Legs

An old woman sat hunched and silent at a large desk. She was as old as a mummified octopus, so old her skin was wrinkled and crinkled from top to toe. Only a few scrags of cobwebbed hair remained on her ancient skull. Her nose was small and flat and her crabby mouth had almost no teeth, just a sprinkling of wobbly, mottled brown stumps. Everything about her seemed to have been made from secrets and shadows, cobwebs and dust.

The old woman was sitting in a motorized wheelchair. She had built it herself, adapting an old tea-trolley. She sat on the top tray, like some strange, large cake, with legs dangling over the front. An electric motor took up most of the bottom tray. Arranged around her were all sorts of controls.

As for the desk, it was piled high with scissors and knives, reels of thread, needles, pins and rolls of sticky tape. Mixed in with all this was a jumble of electrics – small motors, TV tuners, wiring, hard-drives and umpteen other nerdy bits from cannibalized computers.

And then sticking out from among this ragbag
of bits and bobs were –

WARNING!
If you're squeamish,
don't read this bit!

– BODY PARTS. Urrggh! Arms, legs, feet,
hands, fingers, toes, heads, ears, noses, eyeballs –
the whole lot.

Every so often the old hag would start
muttering and rummage through the pile,
scattering junk in her wild search. With a half-
mad, crow-like cry, she would pounce on an

eyeball or maybe a big toe, hold it up, squint at it and settle to work with needle and thread.

What was she doing? She was MAKING MONSTERS! (It was a bit like Lego, but with very different results.)

She was sewing them together, bit by bit – an arm here, a leg there.

Who was she? THE STITCHER!

This dark, dingy dungeon was her home, a cavernous ruin full of creaks and groans, hidden corners, uncountable rooms and endless, crumbling corridors. For years she had sat there, making more and more monsters, while her eyesight grew worse and worse.

It was a shame about her eyes. She had done so much close work she could no longer see properly and she often made mistakes. Her stitching was pretty useless too.

In fact, SHE SIMPLY WASN'T MUCH GOOD AT MAKING MONSTERS.

One monster had both legs on back to front and couldn't see where he was going. Another had one leg facing frontwards and the other facing backwards and could only shuffle round in a small circle. There was an ogre that had a wiggly hand where an ear should have been.

And then there was that shoddy stitching. It was always coming undone. The monsters were falling apart at the seams. Every so often someone's head would fall off and roll across the floor, or maybe it would be their nose, a hand, or a leg – in which case they'd probably topple over. Or perhaps an eyeball would pop out at breakfast and land in someone's cereal.

They would have to drag themselves back to

The Stitcher and she would sew them up again,
until the next time they fell apart.

The Stitcher turned to her trusty helper,
Grumpfart. Poor Grumpfart – her smell was
worse than the most ancient lavatory. Her insides
were constantly bubbling and boiling. Every so
often there would be an enormous eruption and
a volcanic burp would explode from one end,
usually accompanied by a stinking gas blast from
the other. The Stitcher was the only person who

BURRRRP!

could put up with her, possibly because The Stitcher had lost her sense of smell. (And a good thing that was too, because The Stitcher's body odour was not exactly like a flower meadow.)

Now Grumpfart sidled up to her mistress, enveloped as usual in a cloud of poisonous stench. She stood there, a quivering volcano shuddering with mini explosions, belches and hiccups.

'What shall I –' *HICC!* – 'do?' *SPPPPPPPRRRRRRR!*

'Turn on the particle-synthesizer. It is time to bring this one to life,' rasped The Stitcher. She gazed down at the lifeless creation lying across her lap and smiled. 'There, I only have to fit your new brain and then you'll be ready. Hmmmm. And maybe this time I'll have succeeded in removing the Scare Reactor.'

Grumpfart went across to the synthesizer, fizzing and steaming with every step. The big machine was plugged in and powered up. A red light on top began to flash. 'The particle-synthe–' *SPPRRRGH!* – 'synthe–' *SPPRRRGH!* – 'synthe–' *SPPRRRGH!* – 'synthesizer is weady, mistwess.'

The old crone rummaged through the pile on her desk until she found a large saucepan which she connected to the wires on the synthesizer. This would keep the electrical charge circulating in the monster's body. She propped up the monster in her chair and rammed the pan down on the monster's head.

The Stitcher smiled. 'Hmmm. It's time for you to awake, my sweet!' she crooned, and flicked thc switch. Blue sparks zizzed from the plug. The machine began to hum and whirr, getting louder and higher until it was almost screaming. The Stitcher pressed the big red flashing button on top of the synthesizer and at the same moment flung herself beneath her desk.

FFWATTAANNNGGGG!

The wires jumped with the surge of power.

Mini shafts of lightning shot out in every
direction, smashing glasses, shattering cupboard
doors and sending the rats scurrying for cover
under the desk with the old woman. Grumpfart
was blown clean off her feet and went whizzing
through the air with her huge dress blown
right over her head so that you could see her
ginormous green knickers – not a pretty sight.

She landed in the far corner with a loud squelch.

SHHPLOOOP!

The slumped body in the chair jerked and jolted. For a split second you could see the skeleton inside glowing a ghastly green. The monster's hair stood on end and his body suddenly rocketed from the chair, hit the ceiling and stayed there for several seconds, humming with electricity, before crashing back down to the floor. Astonishingly, he landed on his feet and stood there, swaying gently.

The eyes popped open – well, one of them at any rate. The other seemed to be stuck shut. The Stitcher snatched up a broom handle and prodded the head with it until the eye snapped open.

'Hmmmm – that's better,' muttered The Stitcher, switching off the synthesizer and removing the clips. The monster stood there, swathed in clouds of smoke as they drifted from his super-heated body. Grumpfart had recovered from her unexpected air travel and came over to admire the new monster.

'What will it do?' *UURRKKK!*

The Stitcher ignored her and gazed at her new creation. 'There, my dear. And how are we today? Hmm?'

The monster's eyes rested on The Stitcher. His jaw worked up and down. His mouth fell open.

'Muh, muh, muh,' he went, over and over, like a lost lamb, his voice getting louder all the time. 'Muh meee, mummy!'

'Yes, my sweet. That's very good. How do you feel?'

The monster answered in short bursts. 'I – am – jumpy.'

'Hmmm. You've had a bit of a shock,' muttered The Stitcher, and her face cracked a wicked smile. 'About thirty thousand volts,' she added with a cackle.

'What – is – my – name – please?' began the monster, but then his voice suddenly changed and he spoke almost normally.

'*High cloud will move in a westerly direction bringing rain to all parts by the end of the afternoon. Temperatures will be below normal and* – oh – dear – my – head – feels – funny.'

'Hmmm,' said The Stitcher. 'I must have connected a bit from an old television set to your brain and you're picking up the weather forecast.

Hmmm. I shall call you – Weatherman.'

'– *An area of high pressure is moving in from the west bringing more rain on Thursday and there is* –'

'That's quite enough!' snapped The Stitcher, banging the monster's head with the broom handle again.

'Ooooh!' giggled Grumpfart, holding her own noddle.

The monster jerked. 'My – name – is – Weather – man. I – like – that. Thank – you.'

'Hmmm. Now let's test your reactions.' The Stitcher covered her own face with both hands. A moment later she whipped her hands away and shouted – 'BOO!'

Weatherman jumped almost a mile in the air and he burst into tears. 'Please – don't – do – that. I – am – scared. Please – mum-mee.'

The Stitcher groaned and her head slumped forward. 'Another scared monster. Will I never create one that has no fear? What is the point of having monsters that are so easily frightened?'

She turned to Weatherman. 'Listen to me, tin-head. You must never show how scared you are, all right? People will just laugh at you and you are supposed to strike fear into their hearts. Now off you go like a good boy and join the others.'

'Yes – mummy,' croaked Weatherman and he plodded away down the hallway while The Stitcher gazed after him. He'd only taken a dozen steps when his left arm fell off. He bent down, picked it up with his right hand, scratched his head with it and carried on.

The Stitcher didn't notice. 'That's one more,' she muttered. 'Sixty years of work and I'm almost done. Hmm. All I have to do now is complete my masterpiece, or maybe I should call it my monsterpiece! Ha ha ha!' she sniggered. 'And he'd better be fearless. I'm sure I know what to do to his brain. This time I shall get it right and then I'll be ready to take my revenge on the world and let loose ALL my crazy creations!'

And she broke into the kind of horrible cackle you might expect to hear falling out of the crabby, brown-toothed mouth of an ancient crone who held a nasty grudge against the entire world.

'HA HA HA HA HA HAH!'

'*Ha ha ha ha ha hah*' it echoed down the silent, stony corridors of despair.

HOW VERY AWFUL!

3 Back to the Soup Bowl . . .

Ben struggled to heave himself out of the huge
soup bowl. He kept slipping back in. Charlie
thought it the funniest thing ever. His friend's
head would appear at the edge of the bowl for a
few seconds and then suddenly vanish back into
the gloop.

Eventually Charlie offered Ben his arm to grip
on to and Ben managed to drag himself out and
slop on to the floor.

'You're a bit of a
mess,' Charlie observed.

'Really? I hadn't
noticed,' muttered Ben,
trying to wipe
his eyes clear
of soup so

29

that he could at least see.

Charlie didn't like the look of the dank, stony walls of wherever they were. 'What happened?' he asked.

'I fell into some tomato soup,' Ben answered.

'I mean, how did we get here and where are we?' Charlie went on. His eyes were beginning to bulge. He was already wondering what dreadful dangers lurked beyond the dark grey stones of the walls.

Ben tried to wipe sloppy slabs of soup from his arms, chest and legs, but he only managed to spread it around even more.

'It was your Cosmic Pyjamas,' Ben pointed out. 'It was that stupid picture. I touched it and WHAM! BAM! Here we are.'

'Here we are where?' asked Charlie.

'Just a moment, I'll look at the map.'

'What map?' Charlie asked.

'The map I haven't got,' Ben answered heavily.

'How – how are we going to get back?'
Charlie moaned.

'We'll take the bus from the bus stop.'

'What bus stop?'

'The one behind the giant soup bowl,' Ben
went on and to his amazement Charlie began to
walk round to the far side of the bowl. He soon
came hurrying back.

'There isn't one,' he squawked.

'Of course there isn't, jelly-brain.' Ben
couldn't help laughing.

'How will we get back then?' Charlie repeated
with increasing concern.

Ben shrugged. 'Don't know,' he admitted.
'But look at it this way. We got here somehow, so
there must be a way back.'

'Not helpful,' complained Charlie.

'Sorr-ree,' muttered Ben.

They sat down against a mouldy wall and tried
to work out what had happened. It was almost
as if they had travelled through outer space, but

they hadn't been in a rocket or space suits, so surely that was impossible? In which case, what *had* happened? Obviously they were no longer in Charlie's house and, without being able to prove anything, it felt as if they'd travelled hundreds, maybe thousands, of miles.

Charlie had a bruised backside and Ben was covered in tomato soup. They were in a large room with a stone floor, stone walls and a high stone ceiling. There was a thick wooden door in one corner and there was no obvious way they could have got into the room apart from the door, which was shut.

Besides, Ben had fallen straight into the soup and that meant they must have come from above, through a ceiling made of solid stone, which was impossible. It was a mystery they couldn't solve. Their minds were soon taken off the problem by noises from beyond the door. Someone was coming.

Clump, clomp, clump, clomp . . .

It sounded like a giant wearing hobnail boots. Quite possibly a child-eating giant with hobnail boots, one who especially liked tomato-soup-flavoured children. Charlie shot behind the giant soup bowl. Maybe he was hoping to escape by bus. Ben went and joined him and they both prayed for a No. 177 to come along. It didn't.

Clump, clomp, clump, clomp . . .

The door opened and in walked a tall, small child. She was little and grubby, about eight or nine years old, but she had two large tins tied to her feet with hairy string to make her taller, which is why she was both small *and* tall. Her face was pinched and her hair lank and greasy. Ben certainly wasn't scared of *her*, so he popped out from behind the soup bowl.

33

'Oh!' The girl took several steps back, keeping
her eyes on him all the time. 'Is you one of
them?' she asked, with a surprised frown.

'I don't know,' Ben answered. 'Who are *them*?'

The girl looked back over her shoulder
towards the door. 'Them Back There. I ain't seen
you before. What you wearin' all that soup for?'

'I like the smell,' Ben quipped.

'Where did you come from?' the girl
demanded.

'The soup bowl,' Ben answered truthfully.

Charlie decided it was safe for him to come out too. After all, Ben hadn't been killed yet, so Charlie thought it was safe to put in an appearance.

'There's two of you!' cried the girl. 'How did you get in?'

'We were hoping you could tell us,' Ben said. 'One moment we were playing on Charlie's bed and the next I was trying not to drown in the soup. Name's Ben, by the way. He's Charlie. How about you?'

The girl shook her head. 'I don't have no name,' she said quickly. 'Except the ones Them Back There call me – Scumhead, Wormbag, Tin-toes and so on.'

'That's not nice.' Charlie was shocked. 'Suppose we call you Small-Tall, because that's what you are, sort of.'

The girl seemed impressed. 'You's clever, you is.' Charlie lifted his chin proudly, but the girl hadn't finished. 'Except you're wearin' pyjamas, which is weird, if you don't mind me sayin' so. An' they've got funny pictures on 'em.'

Charlie ignored that. 'What is this place?' he asked.

Small-Tall shrugged. 'It's where we are, innit?'

'Yes, but where are we?' Charlie insisted.

'In here, of course! I thought you was clever. Anyways, what you doin' here? Have you come to work?'

'No way!' said Charlie. 'We're going home as soon as we can.'

Small-Tall burst out laughing. 'Are you doolallylilo or somefing? Nobody goes home from here!'

The boys looked at each other with alarm. Were they in some kind of prison? Ben frowned. 'We were hoping you might help. You could tell us where we are, for a start, and who Them Back There are. This is your house, after all.'

'My house? You havin' a laugh? House

of Horrors, this is. Belongs to The Stitcher. Everyone knows that.'

Charlie had turned pale. He didn't like the idea of anyone called The Stitcher. He hardly dared to ask, but he had to know who The Stitcher was.

'She's a nasty old hag-bag, that's what she is. Not that you're likely to see her. She only comes out about once a year, an' when she does you always know she's comin' cos of the smell an' the noise. Grumpfart goes wiv her, see? She's a walkin' cesspit, she is, you wait an' see. An' if you *do* see 'em, you watch out. The Stitcher's Big Trouble. She's the one what makes Them Back There.' Small-Tall nodded to herself.

Ben was losing patience. 'But who,' he began slowly and determinedly, 'are Them Back There?'

'Monsters, of course,' declared Small-Tall. 'Everybody knows that! Where you been all your life? I'm tellin' you, this is a House of Horrors.'

Charlie hurriedly sat down in case he fainted with shock. 'Monsters?' he repeated faintly. 'What – what – what sort of monsters?'

'Oh, you know,' Small-Tall answered casually. 'This an' that.'

'What do you mean?' Ben practically yelled at her. 'What sort of monsters are we talking about?' Ben was dying to know. He reckoned this was the most interesting thing that had happened to him in ages.

'Dunno, bit of a mix, I guess – there's a vampire, Dracolio. An' there's Pizza-Face. He's called that cos his face is so mashed up it looks like pizza toppin'. Then there's 'Andy Mandy – she's a laugh! Got a hand where her ear should be!'

Ben was intrigued. He'd always wanted to meet a real vampire. Charlie, on the other hand, was horrified. How could Small-Tall joke about monsters? She hadn't finished either.

'An' then there's werewolves, bogtrolls,

vampwolves, werepires, boglevamps – mix 'n'
match really. Oh yeah, almost forgot – there's
Headless Harry and his Headless Dog too.'
Small-Tall looked at the boys to see what effect
she'd had on them.

Charlie's legs had gone all wobbly. 'Who, or
what, is Headless Harry and his Headless Dog?'
he asked, with a trembling lip.

Small-Tall shrugged. 'Bit obvious, innit? They ain't got no heads, have they? At least they have got heads, but not on their shoulders. They have to carry 'em. Looks like they've got handbags, really.'

Charlie gulped. Heads being carried like handbags? 'Aren't you sc-sc-scared of them?'

Small-Tall stopped for a moment and thought. 'Not really,' she answered. 'It gets nasty when they shout an' come after me, but I'm too quick. Anyways, I'm the only one who'll speak to 'em. The others is too scared.'

'What others?' asked Ben. 'Who are the others?'

'Kitchen kids, of course. Dozens of us kitchen kids, there are. There's always more kids comin', that's what I thought you was doin'. Them monsters go out and get 'em and we end up here as slaves. That's what we are – slaves, stolen off the streets.'

'That's terrible,' said Charlie, genuinely

shocked. 'Don't you ever try to escape?'

'Are you jokin'?' squeaked Small-Tall. 'Fat chance of escape wiv all them monsters about. An' if The Stitcher found us tryin', she'd monsterize us too.'

One thing still puzzled Ben. 'Small-Tall, why do you wear tins on your feet?'

Small-Tall rolled her eyes. 'Can't do the cookin' otherwise, can I? Can't see them pans proper without these. My idea. I thought of 'em.' She gave the boys a proud grin. 'I fink of lots of fings, I do. You'd be surprised what I fink of. Now, I got to take the soup to the kitchen. You can help if you want. Then you can meet the kitchen kids.'

Small-Tall got behind the giant soup bowl, leaned her shoulder against it and began to push. The boys were surprised to discover there were four small wheels hidden underneath.

'This is their supper.' Small-Tall sniffed. 'An' they're welcome to it too.'

'Hang on a moment,' Ben said, hopping after her. 'I think I've left a shoe and sock in there.'

'Good,' she grunted. 'They'll give it extra flavour.' And they went through to the kitchen.

It was complete and utter bedlam. The noise was extraordinary, impossibly loud and overwhelming.

Charlie and Ben were staring at a steam-filled nightmare.

4 The Grub Tub

Children of all ages rushed about, carrying pans, spilling plates, dropping cutlery, dragging sacks of vegetables.

Everyone yelled at everyone else. Several of the smaller children had tins tied to their feet, like Small-Tall. They were all dressed in shapeless, colourless rags.

Right in the centre there was a stepladder crowned with a small platform. Sitting on top, with his legs dangling over the edge, was a pinch-faced, spotty teenager. When he wasn't blowing screeching blasts down an old, battered trumpet, he was yelling commands through a megaphone made of rolled-up newspaper.

'More potatoes at Saucepan Five!' *BLAAAAAAAAAARRR!* 'Hurry up, skanky pants! Oi! Tiddle-head! You've dropped the bacon again!' *PAH PA-RARRRRR!* 'Come on, get a move on. Them Back There are waiting.' *BLAR BLARRR!!!* 'What are you two mud-brains doing at the door there? Get on with your work!'

Ben made a half-hearted attempt to clear some of the soup from his clothes and nudged Charlie. 'He's talking to us. Act like you know what you're doing.'

'What *am* I doing?' squeaked Charlie, freezing on the spot, while Ben heaved a sack of cabbages on to his back.

'Just look like you're helping,' hinted Ben.

Charlie looked round for something useful to do and, spotting a carrot that someone had dropped, he picked it up and approached some of the children.

'Excuse me, is this your carrot?' he asked. 'Anyone lost a carrot?' They ignored him, pushing him out of the way, until Charlie began to get cross with them.

'This must be somebody's carrot!' he cried.

Ben shook his head and sighed. Charlie had never fitted in anywhere. He'd always stuck out like a sore thumb. 'Charlie, come here! Take the other end of this sack and help me. Honestly!'

'Honestly what?' demanded Charlie, still in a mood.

'Doesn't matter. Keep your head down. We don't want to get noticed. We'll keep carrying this sack round and round. I don't suppose anyone will realize we're not actually doing anything. Don't speak to anyone but keep your eyes open.'

'I won't be able to see where I'm going if I don't,' said Charlie crossly, putting a smile on Ben's face.

'You know what I mean. Look out for any other doors, or anything unusual.'

'Ben, this whole place is unusual, turtle-head.'

Round and round went the boys, taking note of everything – the mess, the noise, the incredible hive of activity. Most of all they noticed the rag-tag children. A few were older than them, but mostly they were a similar age or younger. Working non-stop, they hurtled from one job to the next, urged on by frantic trumpet blasts and bellowed orders from the pimple-faced boy on the platform above.

They slaved away as if their lives depended on it – which quite possibly they did. It was complete chaos. Charlie and Ben were exhausted by just being there in the thick of it. On top of that, alarm bells were beginning to go off in Charlie's brain. He turned to Ben.

'Do you realize where we are? Look around, Ben. What do you see? Child labour – slavery.'

'Oh yeah, I guess you're right. Bit like the Victorian times Crumblebag was banging on about.'

'It's not *like* Victorian times. This *is* Victorian times.' Charlie's face was even paler than normal.

Ben stopped dead and stared all around. His pal was right. In which case –! He grabbed Charlie's shoulder excitedly. 'We've time-travelled!' he cried.

Charlie wasn't excited at all. In fact he was getting more and more worried. 'We're stuck in Victorian times, Ben, in a House of Horrors. I don't want to be stuck here. I want to be at home in my bedroom, in my bed, with a choccy biscuit and a hot-water bottle. It's these jim-jams, these horrible Cosmic Pyjamas. They've done this and now we're stuck and –' Charlie was rudely interrupted by a loud trumpet blast.

PAH PA-RARRRR! 'Oi, you two snails!' yelled Pimples. 'Yes, you two!' he bellowed, pointing at the two boys. 'Get over to the grub tub and take the food up.'

Charlie gulped. Ben shuffled his feet. Neither of them had any idea what Pimples was going on about.

'Don't just stand there! Get on with it!' yelled the boy on the ladder. *BLARR! BLARR!!*

Small-Tall came clomping past on her tins. 'Follow me,' she urged.

Gratefully, the boys fell in behind as she led them across the crowded kitchen to a large hole in the wall, like a fireplace, but without any fire. A thick rope hung down from the shaft above. Attached to the rope was a gigantic basket, divided into two halves. The boys stared at it.

'That's the grub tub, innit?' Small-Tall explained. 'We load up the basket wiv food for

Them Up There, an' you two get in, an' we haul on the rope an' you get carried up that chimney hole until you get to The Grubbery. Then you hop out the basket, get the food an' take it to the table.'

'What's The Grubbery?' asked Charlie, who could feel all his insides slowly cartwheeling down into his shoes.

'It's where we give the monsters their grub, innit?' explained Small-Tall. 'Talk about statin' the bloomin' obvious.'

The boys peered up the dark, dark shaft
that disappeared upward. 'I can't go up there,'
whispered Charlie, boggle-eyed.

'This is our chance, Charlie,' said Ben
excitedly. 'We can go up there and see them –
the monsters!'

'I don't want to see the monsters,' Charlie
answered flatly. 'I want to go back home and
when I wake up I want to find that it's all been a
terrifying nightmare and I'm not wearing these
horrible Cosmic Pyjamas.'

'Yeah, they're strange, them jim-jams,'
muttered Small-Tall. 'I thought they was strange
when I first set eyes on 'em.' She reached out to
touch.

'Don't do that!' cried Charlie.

'What? Why not?'

'You don't know what might happen.'

Small-Tall gave Charlie a suspicious look.
'You're strange, you are. I was only goin' to

touch 'em. I wasn't goin' to rip 'em off or anyfing.'

By this time they had finished loading one half of the basket with big bowls of soup for the monsters and giant chunks of bread. Small-Tall said they'd better get in, sharp-like, or there'd be big trouble and questions asked. Ben scrambled into the seating half and looked at Charlie.

'Come on,' he urged. 'It's cool.'

Charlie climbed up into the basket, very slowly. 'If I die, Ben,' he began heavily, 'I want you to know that I'd like daffodils on my grave. Oh yes, and I also want everyone to know that this is ALL YOUR FAULT.'

'Right,' said Ben, cheerfully agreeing.

'Is he always like that?' asked Small-Tall.

'Yep,' said Ben. 'And he's *still* my best friend.'

Small-Tall called over three of the older children. They grasped one end of the rope and began to haul. In a few seconds the basket had disappeared completely into the dark shaft. The rope creaked and the basket slowly revolved, swinging to and fro and banging against the grimy sides of the shaft.

Ben became more and more excited. 'We're going to see the monsters, at last!' he whispered in Charlie's ear.

Charlie let out a moan. 'I've got a headache and I'm dizzy,' he complained.

'I can see light up above us,' said Ben. 'We're almost there!'

'Great,' Charlie whimpered.

The light from above gradually filled more and more of the shaft until the basket arrived at The Grubbery and hung there, swinging gently. A dirty-faced boy shuffled quickly across to them.

'And about time too,' he grumbled, pulling the basket on to a stone shelf. 'I thought the food would never arrive. Hurry up. You know what this lot are like when they're hungry.'

Charlie and Ben stared into the stony chamber, and there were the monsters, ready,

roaring and waiting, banging their huge knives and forks on the table. It was as if all the boys' nightmares had been collected together and put into one room.

'Charlie!' hissed Ben, shaking his friend. 'Have you fainted again? Charlie!'

5 The Freak in the Fridge

Far away, down many long, dark passageways and in a large, high-ceilinged stone chamber sat The Stitcher. Her wrinkled brow was scrunched into a moody scowl. She was brooding on her miserable childhood.

The Stitcher had never been a happy child. To put things simply, she was a scaredy-cat. She was scared of everything from ants to zombies, and especially zombie ants – the really big ones. It was probably her mother's fault. (The Stitcher's father had been killed in an accident. He had invented the world's first fully automatic vacuum-powered toilet. Unfortunately, when he tested it for the first time, it sucked him down the pan and he was never seen again.) The Stitcher's mother was not a loving person. She didn't go

in for kisses and cuddles and bedtime stories. In fact, she didn't go in for much at all, except telling off her daughter.

'Don't stick your tongue out at me or The Scissorman will come and CUT IT OFF! Stop picking your nose or you'll sneeze giant slugs out of your nostrils for the REST OF YOUR LIFE! Eat your bowl of

cold porridge or Mr Megagob will feed you FISH-HEADS and RABBIT POO for a month!'

The Stitcher's mother had an

endless list of bogeymen she used to scare her little daughter. And The Stitcher was VERY scared. She would hide under her bedcovers, hardly daring to set foot on the floor in case one monster or another grabbed her.

The Stitcher was three when she made her own very first monster. She had been given her first doll and she had quickly decided that it was far too pretty with its blue glass eyes and frilly dress and rosebud lips. So she got a black pen and put spots all over its face. Then she drew on a moustache. When she looked at what she had done she laughed for the first time in her life.

After that The Stitcher pulled off both arms and both legs and swopped them round, so one arm was where a leg should have been and one leg was on backwards. The other leg was where her arm should have been.

Then she sat up in bed, grimly gripping her terrifying creation, holding it in front of her like a magic shield, and for the first time in

her life she began to feel safer. Twisted Dolly
would protect her.

The older she got, the more complicated
her monsters became. She used anything
she could lay her hands on, surrounding
herself with monsters of her own. They were
her bodyguards, her friends, her constant
companions.

But her great dream was to be able to bring her monsters TO LIFE! If only she could do that. At first she thought that all she needed to do was feed them. She would force spoonfuls of porridge into their hard faces, but their heads just got smothered in mush, of course. She made holes in their bellies and poked food inside. The monsters became smeared and greasy. They were plastered with ancient food and stank more than a pile of dead fish.

The Stitcher didn't mind. It made them even more awful and that meant they were even more powerful. But they still weren't *alive*. As she got older The Stitcher's brain was eaten up by the problem of how to make her monsters come alive.

The Stitcher became crabby and nasty and bent double with thinking too hard. She was crabby when she was twenty, more crabby when she was thirty, even crabbier when she was forty. Now she was eighty and so old she had gone from being crabby to being squiddy – all tentacles and venom.

She lived in her House of Horrors, a despairing, dank dustbin of a place, stinking of onion and cabbage. The Stitcher liked to chew on raw onions or cabbages, just as you might suck chocolate. It was here that she had invented her particle-synthesizer and learned how to bring her monsters to life. Now she was plotting her revenge. She hated to see people happy. Most of all she hated children and their laughter.

And now, at last, The Stitcher KNEW! She knew how to make her monsters come to life! She had THE KNOWLEDGE! She had THE POWER! And she had THE MONSTERS! She was already building an ARMY of monsters – Weatherman, Grumpfart and the rest of them. It was an army she would send out into the world to create misery and mayhem. And at their head would be – HER MONSTERPIECE!
DE DE DE DURRRR!!!

It was almost ready and this time it WOULD NOT BE AFRAID! (At least, that's what The Stitcher was hoping.) Only a few details remained. The Stitcher called for Grumpfart and her noxious companion rumbled forward, with a burp here, a belch there and a great deal of tuneless trumpeting from her orchestral bottom.

'What shall I –' *SPPLLLRRURRPP!* – 'do?'

The Stitcher opened her eyes, smacked her lips, pulled out a loose tooth, examined it and pushed it back into her gum with her tongue.

'Open the fridge,' she ordered, and Grumpfart exploded and erupted all the way across the room. A gigantic fridge – although actually it was a freezer cabinet – stood there, reaching almost as high as the ceiling. She pulled on the handle and the door swung open with a hollow thud.

Clouds of icy air came pouring out. As the fog dispersed a shape began to emerge. It was a body. The body of a monster. A monster monster – a monster twice the size of any monster The Stitcher had created before. This was Krankenstein!

DAN-DERANN-DAN-DANNNNN!!!!!

'Bring me my wonder-child!' cried The Stitcher.

Grumpfart took hold of the ropes coiled beside the monster's feet. She bent her back, struggling to pull the giant forward, and the strain forced a gigantic explosion from her body.

SSSSSSSSSPPPPPPPPPPPPPPPPPPPP-SPPPPPPPPPPPPPOOOOOOOPPPPPP!!!!

The juggernaut stood there, tottering, on a wheeled tin tray that rattled and squeaked as it was dragged across the floor. Finally, Krankenstein stood in the centre of the room.

Icicles hung from the freak's clothes. He was encrusted with ice and frost, and he dominated the whole room, such was his immense size. What a GRUESOME GHOUL!

His legs were huge, as thick and powerful as an elephant's. He had rhino-sized feet. His head seemed to be a large bucket. In fact, it *was* a large bucket, upside down and with two round holes for the eyes and a long letterbox slit for the mouth. Most surprising of all was probably the fact that he had seven arms. (The Stitcher had never been much good at counting. She had only meant there to be six.)

But strangest of all, on one shoulder The Stitcher had perched her old, old companion, her first doll. Perhaps she thought it would bring them both luck – bad luck, of course.

The Stitcher eyed her creation from top to toe and she was pleased. 'With this creature I shall terrorize the entire world and make everyone as miserable as I am! Hmmm,' she cackled.

At that moment a nearby door creaked open and a small, grubby face appeared round the edge. The Stitcher arched an eyebrow.

'Is that my little spy? Come in, little spy,

come in,' she rasped and waited while a small
child slipped noiselessly across the room to The
Stitcher's desk, holding her nose.

The Stitcher gazed at the child eagerly. She
pulled open a drawer, fiddled inside and brought
out a bar of chocolate. She placed it carefully on
top of the mess on the desk.

'Now then,' crooned The Stitcher, 'what did
you spy, my little spy, with your little eye? Hmm?'

The child stared at the chocolate with huge
eyes. The Stitcher nudged it closer and licked
her lips. 'Tell me everything,' she prompted.

'Got two visitors, ain't we?'

'Really?'

'Yeah, two kids, older than me, two boys.'

'Hmmm. I don't like boys,' snarled The Stitcher. 'What are they doing here?'

The child shrugged. 'Dunno. One of 'em's still in his pyjamas.'

'Really?' The Stitcher said again. 'Typical boy; lazy, good-for-nothing slop-in-bed. If he doesn't watch out, Mr Spankbott will see to him all right.'

'Yeah, an' they look weird, them jim-jams. Got funny pictures on 'em, they have.'

'Don't you tell me about funny pictures and pyjamas. Reminds me of bedtimes when I was a child. Hmmm. I hate bedtime. My head is always full of nightmares.' The Stitcher shook her scraggy grey locks as if to get rid of some bothersome, biting insects. 'Tell me about them boys. Good workers, are they?'

The child shrugged. 'Dunno how they got

here. They says they was playin' and then, wham bam, they landed in the soup.'

'Hmmm. Two boys, eh?' smiled The Stitcher. 'I could use two boys. I need a couple of victims for Krankenstein. He needs to be tested. Ha ha ha! They'll be just right for my monster to have some fun with. Oh, I am going to enjoy this! Bring me those boys NOW!!'

6 The Monster Munch

Ben shook Charlie hard and patted his cheeks. For a second or two he wondered if he ought to give Charlie the Kiss of Life but quickly decided that would be going Way Too Far, even for a best friend.

'Charlie, wake up!'

Charlie stirred and opened his eyes. 'Where am I?' he began, before remembering he was in The Grubbery, surrounded by monsters. He almost swooned again, but instead he clutched at Ben and pointed wildly towards the table.

'Monsters, Ben!' he squawked.

'Just treat them like they're part of your family,' his friend advised, 'then they won't seem so scary.'

'Ben, my sisters ARE monsters, and they already scare me to bits,' Charlie pointed out.

'This lot are a hundred times worse.'

'All we have to do is feed them,' Ben said. 'Come on.'

They began to ferry the contents of the grub tub to the table. This gave them an opportunity to take a proper look at the diners. They turned out to be a pretty monstrous bunch, even if they were all sporting an unusual collection of headgear – saucepans, tin bowls and, in one case, an old seaside bucket.

Dracolio, swathed in a torn and cobwebbed cloak, was half vampire, half Italian ice-cream salesman. He sat at the table picking bits of carrot out from behind his fang-brace. Handy Mandy was next to him, with her handy car (or car-y hand). Weatherman and Pizza-Face sat opposite.

'Did you see the vampire?' hissed Charlie, as they went back to the basket for more food. 'He had a teeth brace! A vampire, Ben! With a teeth brace?'

'Maybe he's got wonky fangs,' suggested Ben.

'Give me a hand with this soup.'

They carried bowls of soup and bread across to the table. All went well until Pizza-Face demanded more pepper on his soup. 'I want pepper, NOW!' he bellowed at poor Charlie.

Poor Charlie was so nervous he shook the pepperpot until the top came off. Clouds of pepper rose from the monster's bowl and a moment later he gave a monstrous sneeze.

A-A-A-CHOOOOOOOOOOOOOOOOO!!!

Pizza-Face sneezed so hard his nose flew off his face, bounced across the table and landed

with a splosh in Handy Mandy's soup.

'Eeek!' She screamed with terror, glanced nervously at the others and quickly changed her fearful look for one of anger.

'I mean, urgh, how disgusting! Oi! Flatface! Here's your nose!' she yelled, using her spoon to catapult the dripping nose back across the table. It was a lousy shot, which was hardly surprising considering that one of Mandy's hands was attached to the side of her head. The nose went zooming off and this time hit Weatherman.

'This – is – not – good,' he began, before

getting re-tuned into another weather forecast.

'. . . *sunny skies and warm temperatures. Don't forget to wear a hat and have the sun lotion to hand. The north of the country will be higher up than the south and the coast will be wet round the edges.*'

'Will you stop-a going on about the weather before I make-a you wet round-a the edges?' roared Dracolio. He beat his fists on the table until he managed to catch the edge of his soup bowl, sending it spinning into the air, scattering its contents, including Ben's missing sock and shoe, in all directions.

Charlie had backed up against the wall while all this was going on. What with the monsters and the bellowing, he was as white as a cow turned inside out. Meanwhile Ben calmly carried on piling food on to the table.

Charlie wished he didn't feel so scared, but he couldn't help himself. He stayed by the wall, hoping that the monsters wouldn't notice him. But they did.

'Why you not-a working?' roared Dracolio suddenly. 'Bring-a that food here or I stick-a you in-a cornetto.'

Charlie didn't feel like being stuck in a cornetto so he hurried to the table with a pile of sausages. He couldn't help staring at the big pan on Dracolio's head and wondering if it was non-stick or not. And then there was that extraordinary fang-brace.

'Whass-a matter? You no see a brace before?' growled the monster.

'Not on a vampire,' Charlie couldn't help pointing out.

Dracolio grabbed Charlie's wrist. 'You like-a ice cream?' demanded the vampire. Charlie didn't know what to say. What would happen if he said 'yes'? What would happen if he said 'no'?

'Sometimes,' he ventured.

'Of course! Everyone like-a ice cream, Italian ice cream. I make-a you ice cream. You know my favourite flavour? I tell-a you. Boy flavour, with extra chocolato! I make-a YOU into ice cream! Ha ha!'

Dracolio let go of Charlie's wrist and burst out laughing. Charlie gave a weak smile and joined in.

'Ha ha ha,' he said. He felt his blood sloshing into his feet again, along with the contents of his stomach, but Ben was there and pulled him away.

'They're amazing, aren't they?' he grinned.

'Aren't you *ever* scared?' Charlie couldn't help asking.

Ben looked at his friend seriously. 'Charlie, we are in Crumblebag's class five days a week and we have survived. This lot don't scare me, no way.'

Somehow Charlie didn't feel the least bit comforted. And things were about to get far more uncomfortable.

The double doors to The Grubbery suddenly burst open and in came Headless Harry and his Headless Dog. They were, strange to say, instantly recognizable by the fact that neither of them had a head. Well, they *did* have heads, it's just that their heads were not where you expected heads to be.

Harry was holding his noddle by the hair, swinging it from his right hand. As for Harry's dog, the poor creature's bonce lay in a small basket that hung round the dog's neck. Now the pair of them were standing by the door, glaring

at everyone. Headless Harry held his head up
high, like a lantern, so that he could see better,
even though he had an eyepatch over one eye.
(And so did his dog.)

Obviously there was no point in *them* eating
at the table with the others. Anything they ate
would just fall out of the bottom of their heads
and make a mess on the floor. So Double H
and his HD spent all their time wandering the

endless, dark corridors of the House of Horrors, mostly in the hope of being horrible to someone before someone could be horrible to them.

Most of all, Headless Harry liked to announce the arrival of The Stitcher by scurrying just ahead of her, because The Stitcher always – ALWAYS – meant TROUBLE for someone. And Headless Harry liked that. It would have made him laugh his head off if his head had actually been on.

Now a rasping voice and a strange squeaking could be heard coming down the passageway towards The Grubbery, getting nearer and nearer. 'Where are they?' A low growl came from the corridor beyond the door.

'What is it?' Charlie hissed urgently at Ben.

'Wait and see what happens,' Ben answered. 'Stay calm and tell your knees to shut up. I can hear them knocking from here.'

'Hmmm. Where are they? I want to see them,' muttered The Stitcher, and she entered the room, rattling in, perched upon her wheelchair like an ancient grey and crusty cowpat.

'Where are they? Hmmm?' she demanded once more, staring round at the monster-filled room. Her bad eyesight wasn't much use to her here and she turned to her faithful bodyguard. 'Can you see them, Harry? One of them's in pyjamas.'

Harry lifted his head even higher and caught sight of Charlie and Ben, shifting nervously at the back of the room. He brought his head down and whispered into The Stitcher's ear.

She smiled and nodded. The tea-trolley whizzed forward, lurched round the end of the table and zoomed up to Charlie and Ben. Headless Harry was close behind and soon they were joined by Grumpfart, the walking stinkbomb.

'Well, my dears,' crooned The Stitcher. 'Welcome to my humble home. Hmmm. I do hope you are being looked after.'

HICCC! ''Scuse me,' apologized Grumpfart.

'This place is horrible,' Ben declared stoutly, holding his nose. 'There are children here working like slaves in your kitchen.'

SSSPPLLURRRRRRRRRGGGGGGGH!! KRRRRK!

'Oh dear,' sighed The Stitcher. 'How very awful. I must do something about it. What can I do to help? Let me think. I know. I could kill them. That would put them out of their misery!'

'You're a monster!' Charlie blurted, holding his nose too.

PIFF-PIFF-PIFFFFFFFFFFFFFFFFFFFFFFF-FFFFFFFFFPPP!!! 'Oops, sowwy, that was a big one, mistwess. Must have been the soup. Goes through me something wotten, it does. Ooh, here we go again.' *FFFARRRRRRPPPPP!!!!*

'Oh my,' sneered The Stitcher. 'You are a feisty creature, and still in your pyjamas, what a little baby. Cootchy-cootchy-coo! I think baby needs something to play with, don't you, Harry?

And we have a lovely new toy, don't we?'

Both Harry and his canine companion growled their agreement, and Harry flashed a nasty grin at the two boys. 'Krankenstein!' he hissed.

'Oh, wonderful, mistwess!' cried Grumpfart. *URRKKK!* 'Kwankenstein can play with them!'

'See?' said The Stitcher. 'We all think it's a wonderful idea.'

Charlie and Ben had no idea who or what Krankenstein was, but they were both pretty sure that it was something bad, quite probably Very Bad indeed. The other monsters had risen from their dining table and gathered behind The Stitcher. They all stared straight at the two boys. Suddenly the whole room had become very menacing, not to mention smelly.

'What are we going to do?' Charlie whispered.

'I think we'd better scarper, pretty quick,' Ben muttered through gritted teeth.

'I can't. My legs won't move. They've turned

to jelly,' panicked his friend.

'Listen, Charlie, if we don't get out of here right now we shall either be minced by monsters or we'll be fatally poisoned by Farting Flossie over there.'

SSSSSSSSPOPP!

The Stitcher rolled her chair towards the boys. 'Come on, my little playthings. Krankenstein is waiting! Hmmm.'

'Krankenstein can wait forever!' shouted Ben. 'We're off! Byeee!'

He made a brief dash for freedom, realized that Charlie was still rooted to the spot with fear, and whizzed straight back for his friend. The Stitcher was already beginning to claw at Charlie with her crabby hands. Ben yelled at him.

'Come on, Charlie!' Pulling Charlie with him, Ben raced to the hole in the wall and dived into the grub tub. Charlie practically fell on top and a moment later the two were plunging back down towards the kitchen, with the rope whizzing

uselessly through the pulley as the basket went into freefall.

The Stitcher's screams echoed throughout the House of Horrors, calling every monster in the building to her aid, and her words came hissing down the shaft behind them like an avalanche of spears.

'AFTER THEM! DON'T LET THEM ESCAPE! THERE'S A BAR OF CHOCOLATE FOR THE MONSTER WHO BRINGS ME THOSE CHILDREN! BRING THEM TO ME DEAD OR ALIVE! I MUST HAVE THOSE CHILDREN!!'

7 Rescued?

The grub tub went whizzing down the shaft.
Charlie was sure they were about to be smashed
to smithereens. Even Ben was worried.

SPLAPPPPPPPP!

The tub hit the bottom of the shaft with an
almighty bang and burst its sides. The two boys
were winded but otherwise unhurt. Charlie
thought it was a miracle. Ben, on the other
hand, understood immediately what had saved
them. When he had thrown himself into the
basket, he'd landed on what was left of the food,
which was mostly vegetables and fruit.

The food pile had acted as an ultra-squashy
safety-bag when they hit the stone fireplace.
Ben, with the extra weight of Charlie on top
of him, had been pressed very firmly into a

squodgy pile of nosh.

All Charlie had to do was climb off Ben and out of the fireplace. Ben was left to try and unstick himself from all the bits of tomato, bananas, lettuces, strawberries, mashed potato and so on that were firmly stuck to his clothes, along with the tomato soup from his previous landing.

Charlie shook his head. 'You always manage to get yourself into a mess, don't you?'

Ben ignored him. There were more important things to do. 'The monsters will be here any second,' he warned. 'We'd better hide somewhere.'

BLARR-DE-BLAAAARRRRR! It was Pimples and his wretched trumpet on top of the stepladder. 'You two! Get a move on! Washing up to be done!' ***TA-TARAAAAH!!***

The doors burst open and monsters poured into the kitchen. Pans of food went flying up in the air as the monsters waded through the scurrying children, who ran squeaking and squawking in every direction like frightened chickens, trying to escape the fury of the monsters. The stepladder was knocked off its feet and toppled over, spilling Pimples into the seething bedlam, just as he was mid trumpet blast.

Pah-Pa-RAAaaauuuurgle – sqwwwk!

The monsters quickly spied Ben and Charlie. They roared and bellowed, kicking children out from beneath their feet as they closed in on their prey.

'What are we going to do?' asked Charlie desperately.

'Stay calm,' muttered Ben through clenched teeth.

'STAY CALM?' yelled Charlie. 'We're about to get pizzarized!'

'Get ready to run, and follow me,' Ben answered.

'Follow you where?' asked Charlie.

'I don't know,' admitted Ben. 'I'm making it up as we go along.'

Charlie didn't find this very reassuring, but before he could say any more Ben had seized his wrist and was pulling him in his wake.

'Run!'

There may have been several monsters in their path but the two boys had a big advantage.

They were small. They could dodge about so fast that half the monsters were soon overcome with dizziness and either smashed into each other or simply crashed to the ground.

Also, it has to be said that Running was not the monsters' best subject. It's very difficult to run if your legs face in different directions, or they've been put on back to front. It's even more difficult to run if your legs have a habit of falling right off, which is what happened to Weatherman. He went spinning off to one side until he collided with the wall.

'Oh – dear, I – feel – *a cold front moving across the country, bringing low temperatures and rain.*' Weatherman banged his head several times, and then began a hunt for his missing limb.

Meanwhile the chase went on. Charlie and Ben were out through the door and hurtling down a passage. They were closely followed by what sounded like rhinos on the rampage. Charlie cast a frantic look back over his shoulder.

'They're gaining on us!' he panted.

'Run faster!' cried Ben.

'I can't! I've got a stitch.'

'They've got a lot more stitches than you,' quipped Ben, leaving Charlie wondering how Ben could possibly make jokes at a time of such deadly peril. They whizzed round the far corner of the passageway only to come face to face with a wall.

'Wrong turn!' gasped Ben. 'Back the other way. Quick!'

'They're even closer!' cried Charlie. 'We're going to die, Ben. We're going to be torn to bits by manic monsters. I don't want to be torn to bits, Ben. I want to die in bed with a hot-water bottle and some choccy biscuits.'

'Keep going, don't give up!' Ben yelled, but even he was having his doubts. He had no idea where they were going. They could be running straight into even more gruesome ghoulies for all he knew. They rounded another corner and almost sent Small-Tall flying.

'In a spot of bother?' she asked, quickly sizing up the situation. 'Jump in here. I'll sort them monsters out.'

Small-Tall produced a set of keys and quickly unlocked a small door. It was a food store. 'I'll lock you in until they pass an' I'll tell you when it's safe to come out.'

'You've saved us!' said Charlie, and he almost wanted to kiss Small-Tall, but the idea was

still too disgusting to put into action so he kept his lips to himself. The boys piled inside the cupboard and Small-Tall locked the door behind them.

A few moments later the gang of monsters came thundering up. Pizza-Face skidded to a halt and loomed over Small-Tall.

'It's the wrong kid!' he bellowed. 'There were two boys and now there's one girly. What are you doing here, girly?'

'Mindin' my own business, that's what,' Small-Tall answered calmly, and Charlie decided she was very brave. He wished he could be brave too.

The Headless Dog was sniffing curiously at the door and Headless Harry began to take an interest too. 'Why are you standing beside that door?' he demanded.

'Cos it's where I happened to be when you came chargin' roun' the corner like some horse race for elephants.'

Inside the cupboard, Ben sniggered. Charlie

clapped a hand over Ben's mouth.

'My dog thinks there's someone in there,' said Headless Harry, frowning.

'Yeah? Well, that's because your dog is stupid an' can't tell the difference between food, which is what is stored in there, an' children, which ain't what's stored in there. An' anyways, it's locked. Try for yourself.'

The door handle rattled as Dracolio tried to open it. 'It's-a no good. Come on, they must-a go that-a way.'

Inside the cupboard the two boys listened to the sound of departing feet. They waited until the noise had completely died away before letting out their breath.

'Phew!' grinned Ben in the darkness. 'That was a narrow escape.' There was no answer from Charlie. 'You haven't fainted again, Charlie, have you?' Ben asked.

'No, but it's very dark in here and I don't like the dark.'

'At least we're safe,' Ben pointed out. He put his face to the edge of the door and whispered, 'Hey! Small-Tall? Can we come out yet?'

There was no answer, so Ben whispered a bit louder. 'Small-Tall? Are you there?'

Silence.

'Small-Tall! You can let us out now!'

More silence. It was strange how silent silence could be sometimes, and how creepy. They both tried calling for their rescuer, but she had gone.

'What's she doing?' asked Charlie.

'Search me.'

Several minutes passed and still there was no sign of Small-Tall. 'I guess she had to go off with the monsters,' suggested Ben. 'You know, to make it look like she was helping them search for us, or something.'

'Yeah,' murmured Charlie half-heartedly. 'Or maybe they've simply eaten her.'

Ben shook his head. 'We would have heard her scream,' he pointed out, although Charlie wished he hadn't. 'Tell you what,' Ben continued, 'I bet Charles Dickens never had to do stuff like this. I don't imagine he got chased all over the place by farting zombies. At least, if he did, Crumblebag never said so in assembly.'

At least that put a smile on Charlie's face for a few seconds.

Another ten minutes or so went by. They tried the door from the inside but they knew it wouldn't be any use, and they were right. The only light was a faint glow from above. Ben wondered if it came from daylight.

'Maybe it's a way out,' he said, reaching above his head to explore the area with his hands. He managed to knock down several tins and packets of food, including a large bag of flour. It burst over Charlie's head, sending both boys into fits of coughing and spluttering. Ben looked at Charlie and grinned.

'Oops,' he murmured.

'Idiot,' muttered Charlie, brushing the flour

from his clothes. 'Mum'll kill me when she sees this mess.'

Ben chuckled. 'Charlie, there are about a hundred monsters out there trying to kill us and here you are worrying about your mum!' He gazed upward. 'I can hardly see a thing. It feels like there's an open space above and a shelf. See if you can get up there.'

'Why me?'

'Because it might be a bit of a squeeze and you're thinner than me.'

Charlie groaned. This was the sort of adventure that Big Brave Ben should be doing. He was the one who took the risks. Now Charlie would have to do it even though he didn't want to, but he couldn't think of any excuse except '*I'm scared*', which sounded way too pathetic.

'I'll cup my hands together and give you a leg-up,' Ben offered, and a moment later Charlie was being heaved up into unknown territory. 'What's it like?' Ben called after him.

'Like you said, it's a bit of a squeeze,' Charlie answered. 'I'm standing on a stone shelf and I think it goes up further.'

'Can you get out anywhere?' Ben asked eagerly.

'Can't tell. I'll have to climb even higher.'

Charlie scrambled upward and found another small ledge where he could crouch. He still couldn't see any way out. He knelt there, panting a bit from the climb and wondering how they'd got themselves into such a mess. It was because of those wretched pyjamas his mum had given him. He wished he'd never set eyes on them.

Charlie's thoughts were disturbed by noises from down below. It sounded as if Small-Tall had returned at last. He could get back down. Hooray.

Before he could move he heard the lock turn and the door was flung open. Looking down, Charlie could make out the top of Ben's head. And then he saw another head. At least it was

more of a skull, half
covered with cobwebs and
a few scrags of grey-white
hair.

The Stitcher gazed
fondly at Ben. 'What have
we here? Would you like to
come out, little boy? Hmm.
Do come out. I have a little
game to play with you. Do
come out and play.' The
Stitcher rubbed her hands
and spoke much more
sharply. 'Come on. Out!
Out here! Both of you!
You are mine now,
my prisoners!
Hmm!'

8 I Spy, With My Little Eye,
   The Stitcher's Spy

Charlie froze. The Stitcher! His eyes were almost falling out of their sockets as he stared down at the old woman.

The Stitcher grabbed Ben's shoulder with a scrawny hand and dragged him into the passageway. She eyed him from top to toe with disgust.

'What? Only one?' She poked her bony head back inside and looked all around. 'Where's the other one? I thought you said there were two of them?'

Charlie pressed himself back into the shadows, heart pounding. Inside his head he whispered to himself, *Please don't let her see me, don't let her catch me!* And he quickly added: *And please don't let me faint and fall at her feet.*

Another voice spoke and Charlie almost fell off his perch with shock and surprise.

'There was two of 'em. I'm tellin' you, I locked 'em both in. The other one's gotta be in here somewhere cos there ain't no other way out.'

Small-Tall! She pushed into the cupboard and gazed upward. 'See? There's a space up there. How was I supposed to know there's a bloomin' shaft goin' up there? He'll be hidin', I bet. Oi, Charlie-boy! There ain't no way you're gonna

escape. You're trapped an' we'll just come an' getcha so you may as well come out now!'

Charlie stuffed a fist into his mouth to stop himself squeaking with terror. His legs had turned to porridge and he had to press his knees into the corner of the wall to stop them from shaking so much.

'I want that boy now!' raged The Stitcher. 'Krankenstein is waiting!'

Charlie gnawed his knuckles. He couldn't believe that he and Ben had been betrayed by Small-Tall. He pinned back his ears and tried to eavesdrop on the conversation. Small-Tall and The Stitcher were considering action.

'Where does that shaft go?' grunted The Stitcher.

'Dunno,' said Small-Tall. 'Up above somewhere.'

The wrinkled crone pulled a face and copied Small-Tall's voice. 'Up above somewhere. Hmm. OF COURSE IT GOES UP ABOVE, YOU

MINDLESS MOTHBAG! Get up there after him!'

'I ain't goin' up there,' whined Small-Tall. 'It's dark an' everyfing.'

'You get up there,' hissed The Stitcher, 'or I'll get one of those saucepans, pop you in the particle-synthesizer and fix you up just like the monsters.'

Ben suddenly shouted out to Charlie. 'Climb higher, Charlie. Find a way out! You've got to escape before it's too late!'

'You shut your mouth or I'll sew it up!' screeched The Stitcher, but Charlie was already on his way, struggling upward until the walls of the shaft narrowed to such a thin gap that there was no way Charlie could go further. In fact, he was already having nightmare visions of getting stuck there, in the shaft, forever. *And nobody will ever find me*, he thought to himself. *I'll slowly die of starvation and turn into a skeleton and nobody will ever know what happened to me.*

It was such a sad and lonely thought he wanted to cry all over again. He slowly allowed himself to slip back down to the little shelf. He was trapped, doomed and done for.

Down below, The Stitcher hissed at Small-Tall. 'You get up there, double quick, and flush him out.'

Small-Tall flashed a grubby grin at The Stitcher and poked Ben. 'Ain't no need for me to go chasin' Charlie-boy. We got all we need here.'

'If you don't start climbing by the time I've counted to one, it's the saucepan for you,' warned The Stitcher.

'Nah, you listen,' answered Small-Tall, undisturbed by the old hag's threats. 'What we do is this, see. We got Ben-boy, ain't we? So we take him an' we turn him into a monster. You put a saucepan on his head an' make him a monster.' Small-Tall raised her voice to make sure Charlie could hear.

'We'll turn Ben into a monster unless Charlie-boy comes down an' gives himself up. Do you hear that, Charlie-boy? You come down here or your pal gets monstipated.'

Ben was shouting again. 'Don't listen to them, Charlie! Find a way out and escape!'

The Stitcher began to laugh. 'Listen to the darling, trying to save his friend.' She turned to Ben. 'Hmm. You should be thinking about saving your own skin, not Charlie's.'

Ben looked The Stitcher right in the eyes. 'The biggest monster in this place is YOU!' he announced bravely, but it only made The Stitcher cackle louder.

'Ha ha! Oh, no, no. Me – the biggest monster?
You haven't met Krankenstein yet, have you?
But you will, you will. He's – rather tall. Hmmm!
Come on, baby Ben monster. Let's take you to
the particle-synthesizer!' She turned to Small-
Tall. 'Take this rope and tie him to the back of
my chair. I'll set some monsters to guard the
cupboard so if Charlie tries to come back down
he'll get a nasty shock. Hmm.'

Ben trudged wearily up the passage, dragged
along by The Stitcher's motorized tea-trolley.
He eyed Small-Tall furiously.

'You were spying on us and plotting all the time. How could you?'

Small-Tall smiled and answered instantly, 'I like chocolate.'

Charlie heard their footsteps die away, but not before four monsters had taken up sentry duty outside the store cupboard. He crouched down on the tiny stone shelf and wished that he was a billion miles away.

What was he to do now? He was alone in a house full of monsters, not to mention Krankenstein, who sounded like a nightmare on legs. Meanwhile Ben had been taken prisoner and was about to have his brain liquidized. The only way to stop that was for Charlie to give himself up or to think of some way to save his friend.

Charlie almost choked on the bitter truth he was facing. He would either have to try to escape and get back home by himself, or he would have to try to save Ben. Or both. And whatever it was he decided to do, he would not be able to escape the one thing that Charlie had feared most all his life –

THE FEAR OF FEELING FEAR.

It was as if he was born scared and things had got scarier ever since.

No wonder Charlie had slumped into a heap and was holding his head in both hands, trying not to cry even though his eyes stung like mad. He rubbed his eyes with his fists and stared at his pyjamas in what faint light there was. They were the cause of everything. The pyjamas had brought all this misery, whizzing them out of his own home and bringing them to this wretched House of Horrors. Well, those pyjamas didn't look so magical now, dusty with flour and cobwebs. They seemed to spell nothing but disaster and despair.

As that very thought passed through Charlie's

head, the pyjamas really did spell out something, quite literally. Amazing! It was so astonishing and unexpected that Charlie sat bolt upright, the hair on his neck prickling with anticipation and his eyes almost popping from his head.

A tiny thread of softly glimmering letters appeared on his left sleeve, slowly winding between the little pictures of planets and people, animals and mountains.

LOOK IN THE POCKET

That was all it said. *Look in the pocket*. Charlie didn't remember a pocket at all. He patted the jacket all over. No pocket. He felt around the top of the trousers. Still no pocket. He stood up and felt jacket and trousers again, but there was no pocket. Charlie lifted his sleeve. The writing was snaking up to his shoulder now, getting fainter all the time, but it definitely said, *Look in the pocket*, until it vanished altogether.

Charlie sighed. There was no pocket. He sank down, leaning back against the wall, and that was when he felt the lump near the back of his neck. He put a hand to it. There was something there. Something small. Charlie carefully slipped off the jacket and turned it round. Right up near the collar, on the back above the shoulderblade, there was a small pocket. What a weird place to put it! No wonder he couldn't find it at first.

Charlie eagerly dipped his hand inside. There was something in there, something small and soft. Charlie wiggled his fingers around it and carefully lifted it out in his hand. He opened his fingers to see what it was and found himself gazing straight into the small, bright, beady eyes of a mouse.

9 Pizza-Face Loses His Head

A mouse. A small mouse. In fact, it was probably the smallest mouse that Charlie had ever seen, although it did have a rather sweet, long tail. And very pretty pink ears. And neat feet.

'You're going to be a fat lot of good,' Charlie murmured. 'What am I supposed to do with you?'

The mouse sat on the palm of Charlie's hand, looking completely at home and not the least bit afraid. Charlie shook his head in wonder.

'Don't you realize there are monsters waiting for us down below? And if we are lucky enough to get past them, we'll certainly get monstipated by The Stitcher. Aren't you the least bit scared?'

The mouse glanced up at Charlie as if to say, 'No, why should I be?' and carried on cleaning its whiskers.

Charlie sat there, looking at the mouse and wondering what he should do. Quite simply, he wanted to go home. Maybe he had a small chance of escaping the guards and finding a way back. Charlie was beginning to think the Cosmic Pyjamas might help. If the pyjamas could suddenly produce vanishing writing and pockets, then surely they could take him home?

And then there was Ben. Charlie knew, deep down, that there was no way he could abandon his best friend. And that would mean facing the monsters and The Stitcher and any number of saucepans and synthesizers, no matter how scared he felt.

Charlie stared glumly into the darkness. A faint glow appeared near his right knee. He looked down. Some more writing was sliding across his leg. It was a single word:

ELEPHANTS

Charlie was beginning to think the pyjamas were just playing stupid tricks on him. First of all they had produced a mouse and now they said ELEPHANTS. What was the point in —

BOINNGGG!

Of course! Elephants. Mice. The connection! Elephants were supposed to be scared of mice. And if great big creatures like elephants were scared, then maybe the mouse would scare monsters. There was only one way to find out. It was Charlie's only chance.

Charlie carefully put the mouse on his shoulder and told it to stay put while he gingerly climbed down to floor level, as quietly as he could. The door was slightly ajar and, peering out, Charlie

could see Pizza-Face, Dracolio, Handy Mandy and Weatherman. (He'd found his leg and had it sewn back on by this time.)

Charlie cupped the tiny mouse in his hand and held it up to his face. 'Now listen carefully,' he whispered. 'I want you to go out there and scare those monsters silly, but make sure you don't get hurt, all right?'

The mouse looked at Charlie and one eye flicked shut and opened again, almost as if it was winking at him. Charlie grinned. It *was* winking at him. He crouched down and put his hand on the floor by the door.

The mouse sat there for a moment, nose twitching, whiskers all a-quiver. It ran forward a little way, off Charlie's hand and up to the crack in the door. It paused. Charlie's heart began to beat faster, and quite probably the mouse's heart was going at a pace too. There were four ugly, horrible monsters out there. And then the mouse calmly trotted out into the passageway.

112

'AAARGH! AAARGH! AAARGH!' screamed Dracolio, pointing at the floor.

'MOUSE!' yelled Handy Mandy and immediately tried to climb up Pizza-Face as he was the tallest one there. In a few seconds she was sitting on top of his shoulders and clinging to his head. Unfortunately her hand was right over Pizza-Face's eyes so he was sent into a blind panic.

As for Weatherman, he'd gone into jerk-mode, which he always did when he was scared. 'I – am – frigh – tened,' he began, '*but snow will fall and roads are likely to*

be blocked. If you're driving home tonight do make sure you have sandwiches with you in case you get stranded, uhuh, uhuh, in your washing machine. Wazzo makes everything whiter, even your coloured clothes. Use Wazzo for unexpected results. Oh – dear – what – am – I – talking – about?'

By this time the four monsters were charging about in all directions. Pizza-Face kept crashing into the wall or the other monsters because he couldn't see where he was going. Handy Mandy was yelling useless directions at him. Weatherman was now broadcasting a crime-watch programme, while Dracolio danced about on tiptoe as if he was treading on hot coals, and all because there was one tiny little mouse sitting on the floor among them and twiddling its whiskers.

Finally Handy Mandy managed to pull at Pizza-Face's head so hard that it came off in her hand. 'Argh! You idiot! You have pizzarized me! Put my head back on!'

'I'm trying, I'm trying!' cried Handy Mandy, shoving the head on upside down, sideways, nose first – any way except the right one. They both crashed into Dracolio and all three fell to the ground, where Weatherman immediately tripped over them and joined them in creating an impression of a gigantic octopus arm-wrestling itself.

Charlie seized his opportunity, slipping out of the store cupboard and racing up the passageway, but not without quickly stooping to pick up the little mouse on his way.

'Well done!' he grinned, as he shot away from the monsters. 'Now all we have to do is rescue Ben.'

That thought slowed him down a bit. In fact, it slowed him down a lot. Rescue Ben? How was he going to do that? He didn't even know where Ben was. The Stitcher wasn't going to be scared of a weeny mouse. Charlie's feeling of triumph at outwitting the monsters quickly disappeared.

He began to look around him more carefully. The Stitcher could be anywhere and so, for that matter, could Small-Tall. Charlie still found it hard to accept that the little grubby-faced girl who had been so kind to them was actually spying on them all the time and carrying back information about them to The Stitcher.

It was very creepy wandering around the dark corridors and soon Charlie's nerves were so much on edge he almost screamed with alarm when he suddenly caught sight of his own reflection in a cobwebbed mirror. Every corner he came to meant potential danger. He had no idea where he was.

At length he came to a shut door. He thought he could hear voices from the other side but he didn't dare open it. He was standing there, wondering what to do, when several pairs of footsteps came clumping towards him. It sounded like an entire army and Charlie hastily moved round the corner out of sight.

Soon the four monster guards appeared, arguing fiercely with each other.

'You can tell The Stitcher he escaped,' snapped Pizza-Face at Handy Mandy. 'It was your fault.'

'My fault? You lunatic, you were the one who went crashing about all over the place.'

'That was because you pulled my head off!' snarled Pizza-Face.

'*Take your umbrella with you this evening,*'

interrupted Weatherman. '*Rain is forecast for the whole world.*'

'Will you please-a stop-a rabbiting on?' cried Dracolio. 'Your TV rubbish makes-a my brain go like-a messy spaghetti!'

The monsters pushed the door open and clumped in. Fortunately for Charlie, none of them remembered to close it. He crept to the door and peered round.

There was The Stitcher, Small-Tall, at least ten monsters and poor Ben. He'd been tied to a huge wooden chair in the middle of the room. Beside him was a machine with a saucepan dangling from it on lots of electrical wires. Ben looked pale and tired and scared – not at all like the chirpy, cheerful Ben that Charlie was used to.

Well, now it was Charlie's turn to rescue Ben for a change. But how was he going to do that? The room was full of monsters, bogles and ghouls. Maybe the mouse could distract

them, but Charlie doubted it. And it still left
The Stitcher to be dealt with. Charlie swallowed
hard. This was the biggest, most dangerous,
most scary problem he had faced in all his life.

10 The Rebellion Begins

Charlie crept away from the chamber. He knew
he couldn't simply go charging in, expecting to
rescue Ben on the spot. This was something that
would need planning. First of all he needed to
hide out somewhere. The monsters would be
telling The Stitcher about his escape and soon
the whole place would be on the lookout for him.
But where could he hide?

A distant memory floated into Charlie's brain.
It was a story he'd read about a man being
chased by a gang. He escaped by hiding in a
crowd, which surprised Charlie. Surely everyone
would see you? But no – in a crowd you don't get
noticed. You become very difficult to spot.

Charlie decided to hide in the one place where
he knew there would be lots of people rushing

about – the kitchen. He made his way there as quickly as possible and was soon in the middle of the usual hustle and bustle of food preparation. The stepladder was back in place and so was Pimples, ordering all the wretched child slaves about their tasks.

Charlie went and sat in a corner to consider his problem. How could he rescue Ben without it all ending in disaster? Surely there was something he could do to overpower the monsters? He ransacked his brain cells until he'd looked under every single one but he couldn't think of a thing. All that happened was that he ended up feeling even more useless than ever.

He kept staring at the Cosmic Pyjamas in the hope that they would suddenly give him an idea, or maybe another pocket would appear, or at the very least something extraordinary would happen. But no, the pyjamas didn't offer a thing. Charlie began to get more and more cross with them, but then realized how silly he was being. What was the point in talking to a pair of pyjamas?

It was at that point that three panheads came into the kitchen, searching for Charlie. He leaped to his feet, pulled up his collar and set about trying to look busy. He went and stood by the huge sink where washing-up was constantly on the go and pretended to join in.

The monsters wandered up and down the kitchen, casting an eye over everyone, but all they saw were slaves, slaving away. They did a bit of grunting and poking and treading on children to make them squeal, just to show that they were monsters, but eventually they left, empty-handed. Charlie breathed a sigh of relief.

He was putting down the saucepan he had

been pretending to wash when the idea came to him. He thought about the machine he'd seen next to Ben with the saucepan dangling from it, and the wires attaching the pans to the monsters' heads. What would happen if the monsters didn't have saucepans on their heads? Was this what made them work? Would they be able to move at all if they took them off? Would they be able to control themselves? Would they STILL BE ALIVE?

Charlie was beginning to think that he had hit on a good idea. The trouble was that there were a lot of monsters. Did they ever sleep? Surely there'd be guards who didn't sleep? It was a tough job for one small boy to take on. If only he had some help.

That was when Charlie got his second bright idea, and soon he was on his feet and climbing on to one of the big kitchen tables.

BLARRR-BLARRR-BLAAAARRRRRR!

'Oi! You can't climb up there!' yelled Pimples

through his paper megaphone. 'I never said anyone could get on the table. Get off at once.'

'Shut up,' shouted Charlie, 'and listen to me, everyone.'

TA-TARAA-TARAAAAA!!!

'You can't talk to me like that,' bristled Pimples.

'Well, I am,' countered Charlie and carried on ignoring him. 'Stop work, all of you. I have important news.'

BLAH-BLAAOOOOOOOFFFFFFFFFF!!

The battered trumpet suddenly went quiet. Charlie had picked up a large potato and carefully lobbed it down the trumpet, jamming it up. Pimples was so taken aback he just sat and stared at his silenced instrument in dismay.

The children stopped what they were doing and turned to Charlie, who glanced at them nervously before launching into a speech.

'This place is a nightmare,' he told them. 'You are stolen children, working like slaves. Outside

this dreadful prison is a world full of sunshine and freedom. The only thing keeping you here is fear of the monsters. Do you like working here? Do you like being pushed around all the time by those monster bullies?'

'Of course not!'

'Do you want to escape to freedom and go back to your parents?'

'Of course we do!' they answered.

'Good, because there are actually more of you than there are monsters. We can overcome them, and this is how we are going to do it.' Charlie began to outline his plan and slowly the children in the kitchen gathered round him, hooked on his every word. By the time Charlie had finished they were in state of great excitement.

'Do you really think we can do that?' asked a small girl in a scrappy frock and no shoes.

'Yes,' nodded Charlie. 'I wouldn't ask you to do this if we didn't have a good chance of success. But I have to warn you that some of us might get hurt.'

There was a lot of murmuring and then another child piped up. 'We're already getting hurt and it's got to be better than working here all our lives.' And soon they were all repeating that.

'Yeah, it's got to be better than here! Those monsters are always pushing us around.'

Pimples pushed himself forward. 'What are you going to do about Krankenstein?' he demanded and a terrified hush fell on the crowd.

Everyone turned and looked at Charlie.

Charlie swallowed hard. It was very hard to think how to deal with a monster that nobody had actually seen. Everyone had heard of Krankenstein, and they could only imagine what he was like. Their imaginations drew horrible, terrifying pictures in their minds and the children were very afraid.

Inside Charlie's pocket he felt the little mouse give a wriggle. Charlie smiled. He lifted his head and looked straight back at the frightened faces around him. 'Krankenstein is a monster just like the others. He has been made like the others, by The Stitcher. No matter how big he is, he will have the same weakness as the others.'

Charlie reached inside his pocket and brought out the little mouse, nose and whiskers twitching with interest.

'You see this mouse? Do you see how small it is? Just half an hour or so ago this little creature scared off four monsters at once. FOUR

MONSTERS! If one tiny mouse can do that to four of them, just imagine what we can do!'

A murmur of approval ran through the crowd. It grew and grew until it became an excited babble. Soon the children were laughing and shouting at each other.

Charlie looked at the sea of excited faces and realized that he had a small army ready to help him. Inside he was grinning like mad and for now all his fear seemed to have vanished.

'We wait until midnight,' he told his new army. 'Carry on as usual, as if nothing has happened. And tonight we shall strike, when most of the ogres are snoring their heads off.'

As Charlie's new-found friends went back to scraping pans and boiling cabbages, Charlie curled up in a corner and took a break. He was feeling quite upbeat. He wondered if this was how Charles Dickens had felt when he tried to save child slaves. Charlie went on musing for a few seconds and then he was asleep. He was going to need all his wits and energy for the night.

He was woken by a shake. Pimples was standing over him.

'You stuffed a potato down my trumpet,' he said, miffed. 'And I can't get it out.'

'Sorry,' muttered Charlie. 'You were too noisy. It wasn't anything personal.'

'Nobody's ever escaped from The Stitcher and her monsters,' Pimples went on huffily. 'Can't be done.'

Charlie yawned. 'Has anyone ever tried?'

'No, but –'

'How do you know it's not possible then?' Charlie asked, surprised at how forward he was becoming. Maybe it was because he'd managed to escape from the monsters earlier.

Or perhaps it was because he had come to understand the difference between himself and Ben. Charlie never even tried to do anything that he thought was scary or difficult. Ben *always* had a go. Sometimes he failed. Sometimes he got hurt. And sometimes neither of those things happened and he succeeded. It was worth the risk and, besides, he couldn't go home without Ben.

Pimples pursed his lips and shook his head. 'I think you're mad,' he muttered.

'Yes,' agreed Charlie. 'You're right. I'm scared too, but I'm not nearly as scared as I was when I thought I was all on my own. So, are you going to join us?'

A smile crept on to the big boy's face. 'Yeah,' he said. "'Course I am. Wouldn't miss it for the world. And I reckon it's midnight – that's why I woke you.'

'Great! So, let's see if we can get that spud out of your trumpet. We're going to need that.'

While they successfully restored the trumpet, Charlie and Pimples discussed what their tactics should be for their attack. Finally Charlie went to the kitchen door and summoned his troops. The kitchen warriors swarmed round him, the smallest ones clattering about noisily on their tin shoes.

'You can take those off for a start,' ordered Charlie. 'Our attack has to be a surprise.'

Finally all was ready. Charlie stood at the kitchen door and took a deep breath. 'Do you remember what to do?' he asked.

'Yes!'

'Are you ready to do it?'

'Yes!' they repeated eagerly.

'What's the most important thing to remember?' demanded Charlie.

'SILENCE!' they roared. Charlie hurriedly put a finger to his lips. 'Silence,' they whispered.

'OK, follow me,' Charlie ordered, and one by one they crept out of the kitchen and headed for The Stitcher's Chamber of Horrors.

11 Explosions, Fanfares and, Finally – KRANKENSTEIN!

They massed outside The Stitcher's room. Charlie could feel his heart galloping like a mouse with a cat on its tail. He wondered if it was possible for ten-year-olds to have heart attacks. He decided it was more than likely, if they were in his situation. His fear was returning but at the same time he was gripped with excitement, unable to do anything except follow his own instructions.

'You know what to do,' he whispered to his motley army. 'I'm going inside. Hopefully they'll be sleeping. I'll start work on the nearest monster. I'll give you a signal if it's clear. Unplug as many wires as you can. If it looks like I'm about to be captured, then rush in and we'll just have to fight things out with them.'

The rag-bag army gave a collective gulp and hoped that all the monsters would be asleep. Charlie eased the door open and peered in. Monsters lay all over the place, propped against each other, lying on tables or crumpled in corners. Loud snores rumbled round the room like a thunderstorm that was closing in. Only Grumpfart lay alone in a mouldy corner, gently piffing.

Charlie slipped into the room, his eyes searching for The Stitcher and Small-Tall. He soon spotted the old crone, sprawled forward across her desk and fast asleep, but there was no sign of her traitorous little spy. That could be a problem.

Then Charlie saw Ben, still tied to the great chair, but surrounded by monsters. They had placed the synthesizer right next to him and a saucepan all wired up and ready to go. Ben's sleeping head lolled forward, open-mouthed, with his tongue flopping out.

Charlie got on his hands and knees and crawled towards the monsters. He muttered to himself in his head. *I am not afraid. I am NOT afraid. I might FEEL afraid, but I'm not really. I might LOOK afraid, but I'm not really.*

He edged closer and closer towards Pizza-Face, sleeping with a finger stuck up one nostril and green froth bubbling out of the other. Charlie shuddered. *Actually, I AM afraid.*

*I don't mind admitting it. I am so VERY, VERY
AFRAID I shall probably wet myself. I want to go home,
but I can't leave Ben here.*

Charlie crouched down beside the snoring
shocker and carefully unplugged as many wires
as he could from the saucepan attached to Pizza-
Face's head. He glanced back at the door and
signalled to the others to come in and start on
the other monsters.

Soon the room was full of kitchen kids, quietly pulling out leads or simply rearranging them. Little by little they edged towards Ben until at last Charlie was beside him. There were still a few monsters that needed reprogramming, but Charlie was triumphant that he had got this far. All he had to do now was wake Ben up without disturbing The Stitcher or any of the others.

He carefully set about untying Ben but had only done one arm when a pinched face slid out from behind the chair and grinned at Charlie.

'Well, ain't you the clever one, Charlie-boy?' hissed Small-Tall. 'Nah, not really. Did you really fink you could escape The Stitcher, an' take all them kiddies with you? I don't fink so! There's all these monsters behind me you ain't touched yet, an' The Stitcher too, an' all I have to do is wake 'em up wiv one shout.'

Charlie didn't waste time thinking of an answer. With a lightning move he grabbed the saucepan beside Ben and rammed it on to

Small-Tall's head. At the
same time his other arm
shot out and pressed the
red button on the humming
synthesizer.

FWATANNNGGGGGG!

Small-Tall almost hit
the ceiling, hovered there
briefly with a ghastly
green glow and then
crashed back down on to
Ben's lap, waking him at
once. Ben's head jerked
up and he opened his
eyes.

'Charlie!' he yelled.
'You came back for me!'

And, of course,
everyone who was asleep
woke up.

There was instant

chaos! The monsters stumbled to their feet. If
they weren't tripping over the ones that had had
all their wires removed, they were crashing into
each other, hitting out wildly and tugging at
anything that got in their path. Stitching quickly
unravelled in all directions.

'I make-a ice cream of you all!' thundered
Dracolio. 'Big-a ice cream!' And then both his
arms fell off. He stared at them lying on the
floor and then set up a wail. 'Oh, mamma, I'm
armless!'

Grumpfart was in such a state of panic her
bodily explosions had taken over entirely.

SPPPPPPPPPPPRGH! PIFFFFFFFFFFF! 'Oh
dear!' *URRRRKK! HICC! HICC! HICC! SPLUUU-
UUURRRRRRRRRRRRRRRRRRRRRRRRRRRPPPP!!!*
'Oops! Pardon!'

As for Weatherman, he had been
completely re-tuned and was now picking up
advertisements. *'Dumpers disposable nappies now have
Ping-String to give that extra bit of elastic for even more
comfort. Use Dumpers, the only nappy with Ping-String.'*

TA-TARA-TATA-TARARRRR!

Pimples's trumpet had never sounded so splendid. Urged on by trumpet calls, the kitchen kids hurled themselves at the ogres. Soon the monsters that were working properly found themselves having to deal with all the monsters that weren't.

A battle was taking place, with monster struggling against monster. Meanwhile, the children swarmed all over them, tripping them up, climbing up their backs and blindfolding them and generally adding to the noisy confusion. Small-Tall was back on her feet and wandering around in a complete daze.

'Have you any chocolate?' she kept asking everyone, friend or foe, while the battle raged around her. 'I'd really like some chocolate.'

BLARR-DE-BLARRR! 'Get that big one over there!' yelled Pimples. 'Watch out behind you, Charlie!' ***TA-TA-TA-TAHHH!!***

And in the midst of all this, arms, legs, heads

went flying in all directions. Ears whizzed across the room like mini UFOs. Noses got squashed underfoot. Ogres fell in every direction. It was all going amazingly well.

UNTIL THEY HEARD THE STITCHER!

'Fools!' she screamed, suddenly waking in her chair and sitting bolt upright. 'Do you think you can escape? Do you think I only have these puny, useless monsters at my command?' She thrust her tea-trolley into top gear, shot across to the freezer and yanked open the door.

'BEHOLD! Krankenstein!!'

12 The Stitcher Gets Cooking

Clouds of ice-air billowed from the fridge, filled with an eerie blue light. And out stepped the colossal Krankenstein. His legs were as massive as an elephant's. His seven arms were like the deadly tentacles of a huge octopus (but with one missing). His head was a mighty, upturned bucket.

'Go!' screeched The Stitcher. 'Go and spifflicate the lot of them! And start with that wretched child right there!' The Stitcher pointed a thin, bony finger directly at Charlie.

Krankenstein slowly turned towards Charlie. He took his first step. He took his second step. He was closing in. What a monster! He towered over everything. His thunderous steps made the entire building shake. Charlie began to back

away. He couldn't think what to do. As a last resort he pulled the little mouse from his pocket and held it in front of him. Krankenstein took no notice.

The Stitcher screeched triumphantly. 'At last I have created the monster of all monsters, a monster who is scared of nothing. With Krankenstein by my side I shall take over THE

WHOLE WORLD! Ha ha!'

TA TA-TA TA TARRRRR! went Pimples and
his trumpet. 'Get the rope!' he bellowed down
his paper megaphone at the troops. 'Wrap it
round his feet!'

The kitchen kids quickly untied Ben and then
rushed forward with the rope. Now they whizzed
round Krankenstein's enormous feet, round and

round, tighter and tighter until, with his next step, Krankenstein tripped. He fell.

It was like watching a skyscraper collapse. Slowly at first, but then faster and faster and with more and more noise. He toppled forward until finally he crashed against the wall. The ancient bricks crumbled and gave way as the monster demolished half the wall.

Off came his head. Four of his arms fell off and he was left, stunned, still and silent on the rubble-strewn ground. Light from the world outside poured into the House of Horrors, lighting up every dingy corner.

'Noooooooooooooooooooo!' shrieked The

Stitcher, as she was overwhelmed by
cheering kitchen kids. 'My wonder-
child!'

It was over. Charlie and Ben
hugged each other, filled with
relief and triumph. They
hugged until they thought
it was getting too soppy
so they stopped and
just gazed at each
other with silly
grins and a lot of
embarrassment.

The kitchen

kids couldn't believe they had been so successful. They had fought monsters and won! Monsters! No more washing-up. No more potato peeling and carrot scrubbing. No more toiling over huge pans of boiling water and working with hot ovens. They had stood up to the monsters and now they were free!

Within minutes they had taken over the building. They found a switch in the fuse box that turned on all the lights. The place was suddenly flooded with brightness, light that made the monsters cringe and squirm – that is, if they had any limbs left to cringe and squirm with.

The children marched the captured monsters and The Stitcher down to the kitchen and ordered them to set about cooking a feast for them. Pimples climbed back on his stepladder, barking orders down his megaphone and blowing his trumpet.

BLARRR! BLARRRR!! 'Get those spuds peeled, you lazy vampire! Oi! Pizza-Face, throw those cabbages out and bring us something decent to eat!'

As for Small-Tall, she was still wandering about asking for chocolate. They left her alone. The kitchen kids had never been so happy, nor as pleased, and they kept thanking Charlie and Ben for what they had done.

This was nice for the boys, but they had something more important on their minds.

'I want to go home, Ben,' Charlie told his friend.

'Me too. I'll tell you something, Charlie, I was frightened in there. When I was tied in that chair, on my own. I was really scared because you weren't there and I didn't know if you'd come back for me.'

Charlie grinned. He couldn't think what to say, so he kept quiet, but inside his heart was bursting again, and this time it was because he was so pleased, and proud of himself too.

'I still don't know how we're going to get

back,' Charlie said eventually. 'I think everything depends on these pyjamas.' He quickly explained what had happened when he was hiding, with the magic messages. He showed Ben the little mouse too.

'But I still don't know how we're going to get back,' he repeated. 'We're stuck here.'

The mouse sat on the palm of Charlie's hand, washing its whiskers. When it finished, it ran up Charlie's sleeve.

'Where's it off to now?' Charlie wondered.

'Look!' cried Ben. 'Right where it's sitting. That picture is flashing.'

'What picture?'

'The one of that building THERE that looks like YOUR HOUSE!' Ben yelled excitedly.

They bent over the pyjamas. A small building was trembling with light. Charlie was gobsmacked. 'Ben, that IS MY HOUSE!'

'I KNOW, YOU PLONKERNOODLE! I JUST TOLD YOU!' screamed Ben. 'WHAT

DO WE DO?!'

Charlie grabbed his friend. 'Quick, hold on to me tight!' He screwed up his face, reached out with one finger and stabbed at the picture.

BANGGG! KER-RANNGGG!! PHWOOOOO-SSHHH!!!

Colours swirled and whirled past them as they tumbled and rolled through space. Was it space? Who knows. There was no sound, just

rushing colours and everything spinning around them until –

BOMMMMFFFFFF!!!

They suddenly landed with a dull thud on Charlie's bed.

They lay there for a few seconds, half stunned and half wondering if what had happened had really happened. They stared round the little bedroom, mentally checking everything, just to make sure it really was Charlie's room. Wall with Spiderman poster? Check. Several pairs of underpants lying on the floor? Check. Torn curtain from a pretend sword fight gone wrong? Check. It was definitely Charlie's bedroom.

Ben grinned at his friend. 'Hey, Charlie, I'll tell you what. We've got our homework to do still, and we've got a cracker of a story to write for Crumblebag!'

Charlie got to his feet. He had something important to do first. He went straight to his clothes cupboard and found an old pair of pyjamas. He slipped out of the Cosmic Pyjamas and put on the old ones. Then he took the new ones downstairs and told his mother he didn't want them any more.

'They're a bit babyish,' he said.

'Oh, all right. I guess you're just getting so grown up these days. I won't be able to recognize you! I'll send them to your little cousin, Rosie. I expect she'll like them.'

12 and a bit   What Happened Back at School

Mrs Rumble had read all the stories the children had written over the weekend. She was passing them back with her comments.

'Lavinia, well done. I'm sorry your father broke his leg. Thomas, that was a great story. I liked it when you ate the cake. Ah, yes, Charlie and Ben. You've both written the same story. You were supposed to write stories of your own.'

'But it happened to both of us, Mrs Rumble,' Charlie explained.

'No, Charlie, it didn't happen at all. If you expect me to believe all that twaddle about monsters with heads that come off, not to mention unidentified flying ears whizzing through the air, then you must think I am very stupid indeed. Don't think you can get round me by writing about my assembly on Dickens and child labour, either. You will both stay in at break-time and write proper true stories.'

Ben and Charlie were annoyed. Charlie tried to change his teacher's mind. 'But, Mrs Rumble, I can prove it really happened. Look.'

He reached into his pocket and brought out a small, furry creature with bright, beady eyes, a long tail, pretty pink ears and neat feet.

Mrs Rumble sighed. 'Charlie, I am not afraid of mice. It won't work, and pets aren't allowed

in class, as you well know. I will see you both at break-time.'

Charlie sighed. Life really was not fair at all.

Ben gave his friend a gentle poke. 'I bet Mrs Rumble could have beaten Krankenstein any day,' he whispered.

Later, at break-time, the two boys sat in class, listening to the other children playing outside. Charlie was writing out one hundred times I MUST NOT BRING MICE INTO SCHOOL. Ben was working on a 'true' story.

One day I went home from school. I had some tea. It was fish and chips. I watched some television. I went upstairs. I got into bed. I went to sleep. The End.

He showed it to Charlie and shrugged. 'Well,' he said. 'It *is* true.'

Watch out for the next amazing
adventure of the
COSMIC PYJAMAS!

'They're –' *SPLRRRGH!* – 'the best –'
PIFFFFFFFFFFFFFFF! – 'books ever!' –
Grumpfart (aged forty-two and three-quarters)

14½ Things You Didn't Know About
Jeremy Strong

★ ★ ★ ★ ★ ★ ★ ★ ★ ★ ★ ★ ★ ★ ★ ★ ★ ★ ★

1. He loves eating liquorice.

2. He used to like diving. He once dived from the high board and his trunks came off!

3. He used to play electric violin in a rock band called THE INEDIBLE CHEESE SANDWICH.

4. He got a 100-metre swimming certificate when he couldn't even swim.

5. When he was five, he sat on a heater and burnt his bottom.

6. Jeremy used to look after a dog that kept eating his underpants. (No – NOT while he was wearing them!)

7. When he was five, he left a basin tap running with the plug in and flooded the bathroom.

8. He can make his ears waggle.

9. He has visited over a thousand schools.

10. He once scored minus ten in an exam! That's ten less than nothing!

11. His hair has gone grey, but his mind hasn't.

12. He'd like to have a pet tiger.

13. He'd like to learn the piano.

14. He has dreadful handwriting.

And a half ... His favourite hobby is sleeping. He's very good at it.

Ask Jeremy

Of all the books you have written, which one is your favourite?

I loved writing both **KRAZY KOW SAVES THE WORLD – WELL, ALMOST** and **STUFF**, my first book for teenagers. Both these made me laugh out loud while I was writing and I was pleased with the overall result in each case. I also love writing the stories about Nicholas and his daft family – **MY DAD**, **MY MUM**, **MY BROTHER** and so on.

If you couldn't be a writer what would you be?

Well, I'd be pretty fed up for a start, because writing was the one thing I knew I wanted to do from the age of nine onward. But if I DID have to do something else, I would love to be either an accomplished pianist or an artist of some sort. Music and art have played a big part in my whole life and I would love to be involved in them in some way.

What's the best thing about writing stories?

Oh dear – so many things to say here! Getting paid for making things up is pretty high on the list! It's also something you do on your own, inside your own head – nobody can interfere with that. The only boss you have is yourself. And you are creating something that nobody else has made before you. I also love making my readers laugh and want to read more and more.

Did you ever have a nightmare teacher?
(And who was your best ever?)

My nightmare at primary school was Mrs Chappell, long since dead. I knew her secret – she was not actually human. She was a Tyrannosaurus rex in disguise. She taught me for two years when I was in Y5 and Y6, and we didn't like each other at all. My best ever was when I was in Y3 and Y4. Her name was Miss Cox, and she was the one who first encouraged me to write stories. She was brilliant. Sadly, she is long dead too.

When you were a kid you used to play kiss-chase. Did you always do the chasing or did anyone ever chase you?!

I usually did the chasing, but when I got chased, I didn't bother to run very fast! Maybe I shouldn't admit to that! We didn't play kiss-chase at school – it was usually played during holidays. If we had tried playing it at school we would have been in serious trouble. Mind you, I seemed to spend most of my time in trouble of one sort or another, so maybe it wouldn't have mattered that much.

It all started with a Scarecrow

Puffin is well over sixty years old.
Sounds ancient, doesn't it? But Puffin has never been
so lively. We're always on the lookout for the next big
idea, which is how it began all those years ago.

Penguin Books was a big idea from the mind of
a man called Allen Lane, who in 1935 invented
the quality paperback and changed the world.
**And from great Penguins, great Puffins grew,
changing the face of children's books forever.**

The first four Puffin Picture Books were hatched in 1940 and the
first Puffin story book featured a man with broomstick arms called
Worzel Gummidge. In 1967 Kaye Webb, Puffin Editor, started the
Puffin Club, promising to **'make children into readers'**.
She kept that promise and over 200,000 children became
devoted Puffineers through their quarterly installments of
Puffin Post, which is now back for a new generation.

Many years from now, we hope you'll look back and
remember Puffin with a smile. **No matter what your age
or what you're into, there's a Puffin for everyone.**
The possibilities are endless, but one thing is for sure:
whether it's a picture book or a paperback, a sticker book
or a hardback, **if it's got that little Puffin
on it – it's bound to be good.**